Dear Bear

Joanna Harrison

Picture Lions

An Imprint of HarperCollinsPublishers

For James,
Katie
and Hugo.
× × ×

With special thanks to my daughter Katie, aged six,
for writing and illustrating Katie's letters to the bear.

First published in hardback in Great Britain by HarperCollins Publishers
Ltd. in 1994.
First published in Picture Lions in 1994.
This edition published in 1999.
1 3 5 7 9 10 8 6 4 2
ISBN : 0 00 664361 2
Picture Lions is an imprint of the Children's Division,
part of HarperCollins Publishers Ltd.
Text and illustrations copyright © Joanna Harrison 1994
The author/illustrator asserts the moral right to be identified as the author
and illustrator of the work.
A CIP catalogue for this title is available from the British Library.

Printed and bound in Singapore by Imago

Katie liked having tea parties, it meant she didn't have
to think about the bear.

Well, she didn't think about him that much. After all,

she didn't worry when she was busy

at home

and she could even laugh about it at school.

But when she was at home in bed, however hard she tried, she couldn't stop thinking about the bear who lived under the stairs. She had never seen him but she knew he was there just waiting to jump out and grab her.

Sometimes huge bear-like shadows would chase her up
the stairs. Katie decided to tell her parents about it.

She tried her dad but he
was too busy hoovering.

Her mum said, "Why don't you write
him a letter and tell him to go away?"

So Katie took out her pencils and paper and wrote the bear a letter.

She put it in an envelope

and left it outside the cupboard door.

This is what it said

The next morning the letter had gone. In its place was another one. It was addressed to Katie. It read

UNDER THE STAIRS

DEAR KATIE,
                I HAVE
TAKEN YOUR ADVICE
AND GONE AWAY.
        I AM MUCH IN NEED
OF A HOLIDAY FROM
SITTING IN THE CUPBOARD
ALL DAY
                lOVE FROM
                    BEAR xx

P.S. BACK MONDAY.

KAT

During the next few days

Katie couldn't stop thinking

about the bear

on holiday.

On Monday Katie didn't want to come home from school.

When she arrived home she found a parcel in front of the cupboard door. Katie opened it up.

Inside was a little glass dome that filled with snow.

With it was this card

DEAR KATIE,
JUST A LITTLE
PRESENT I BOUGHT
FOR YOU WHILE
I WAS ON HOLIDAY
LOVE FROM
BEAR xx

P.S. IT'S NICE TO BE BACK.

Katie showed her dad. "How generous,"
he said. "Why don't you write him
a thank you letter?"

After Katie had written her letter she put it in
an envelope and dropped it over the bannisters.

It read

Dear Bear Thankyou
for my present.
love from
Katie x
Here it is on my
piano.

The next day there was no reply...

or the day after...

or the day after that.

Katie started to worry about the bear so she wrote him a letter.
This is what it said

The next day she received this reply

Katie rushed to show her mum.

Her mum was very concerned.

"We'll make him a hot-water bottle,

some sandwiches

and a nice cup of tea."

Katie knocked on the cupboard door. "Dear Bear," she whispered, "are you all right?" There was no answer.

The next morning the tray was gone. In its place was a letter.

Katie read the letter to her parents. But they didn't
seem to be listening.

Katie spent all the next afternoon getting ready for her tea

with the bear. She put on her best party outfit

and even brushed her hair.

But when four o'clock came she wasn't so sure she wanted to go. After all he was still the bear in the cupboard.

"Go on," said her mum, "he'll be expecting you."

And...

...he was.